12 THINGS TO DO BEFORE YOU CRASH AND BURN

JAMES PROIMOS

12 THINGS TO DO BEFORE YOU CRASH AND BURN

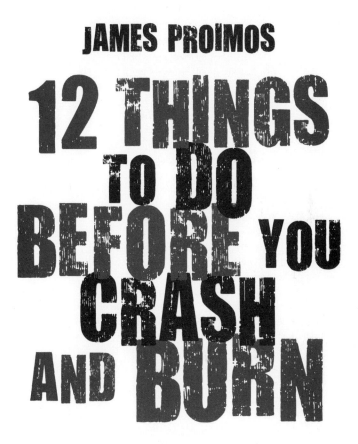

Roaring Brook Press
New York

Text copyright © 2011 by James Proimos
Published by Roaring Brook Press
Roaring Brook Press is a division of
Holtzbrinck Publishing Holdings Limited Partnership
175 Fifth Avenue, New York, New York 10010
macteenbooks.com

Library of Congress Cataloging-in-Publication Data
Proimos, James.
    12 things to do before you crash and burn / James Proimos.
        p. cm.
    Summary: Sixteen-year-old James "Hercules" Martino completes twelve
tasks while spending two weeks in Baltimore with his Uncle Anthony,
and gains insights into himself, his uncle, and his recently deceased
father, a self-help author and daytime talk show host who was beloved
by the public but a terrible father.
    ISBN: 978-1-59643-595-7 (alk. paper)
    [1. Self-perception—Fiction.   2. Fathers and sons—Fiction.
3. Uncles—Fiction.   4. Grief—Fiction.   5. Baltimore (Md.)—Fiction.]
I. Title.   II. Title: Twelve things to do before you crash and burn.

PZ7.P9432Aaf 2011
[Fic]—dc22

                                                    2010043935

Roaring Brook Press books are available for special
promotions and premiums.
For details contact: Director of Special Markets, Holtzbrinck Publishers.

First edition 2011
Book design by Jay Colvin
Printed in the United States of America
by RR Donnelley & Sons Company, Harrisonburg, Virginia

3   5   7   9   10   8   6   4   2

For
Nancy Mercado
and
Baltimore

There is a jar of pickles. No one can open it. The grown-ups pass it around the table. Each one tries to open it. Each one fails. My dad goes next. He tries with all his might. His face goes red. But he cannot open the jar of pickles. He passes the jar to me. I must be about six years old. I grab it and twist as hard as I can. And it opens.

"Hercules!" my dad yells. "You did it!"

Since then, the name has stuck.

Like a jar of pickles, tightly sealed.

1

The casket is closed. It was a plane crash, after all.

The pews overfloweth. As do the sentiments of the never-ending line of avid admirers, casual acquaintances, business associates, relatives, and what have you that take their turn at the podium on the church stage.

One person leaves, another takes his or her place. It's been going on for hours.

A chubby lady wobbles to the microphone:

"He was as fabulous as a man could be. He was rich, but he was charitable. He was strong, he was sensitive. I was lucky to know him. We were all lucky to know him."

She wobbles off.

A tall man in a black suit with a big red bow tie sprints up to the pulpit:

"He was a god. A god, I tell you."

He sprints back to his seat.

An entire family, one of them holding a crying baby, gets up there and sings "The Wind Beneath My Wings."

Now the whole place is bawling.

There is a long silence.

Suddenly, all eyes turn to me. I seem to be the last person who might have something to say.

I slowly walk up to the front of the church. I stand at the podium. I clear my throat.

"He was an ass. My father was a complete and total ass."

2

My mother is a wreck. She has been for weeks.

"I'm sending you to Uncle Anthony's for the rest of the summer."

"Hell no," I say.

"Herc, there's only two weeks left! For once can you just do what the hell I ask you without giving me a load of shit?"

That was the first time I had ever heard my mother say the words "hell" and "shit" in my sixteen years of life. She's basically a saint. And I've never made things easy for her. It was simpler to take things out on her than on my dad.

But it wasn't her swearing that made me back down and go to my uncle Anthony's without a peep.

It was the look in her eyes.

3

I order a hot chocolate in the café car. It reminds me of when I was a kid. I loved riding the Amtrak back then. Not so much today.

When I was little my mom and I would ride the train to D.C. all the time. She would take me to all the museums. Good times, good times.

This trip I will be headed to a town as boring as mud on a stick. I will be seeing my uncle Anthony, who is a good guy and an ass all rolled into one dude. Our way of showing we care is by insulting each other. This is not an uncommon practice among the males of our species.

The guy works all day and goes straight to bed after dinner. I was under the impression that lifetime bachelors had fun 24/7. I would. Not Anthony. He is a different kind of lifetime bachelor. Last time I stayed there for an extended period of time I nearly croaked of boredom. Bad times, bad times.

The train isn't crowded and I could have two seats all to myself. But I take an open aisle seat next to a very pretty girl. She looks older. Probably in college. She's got books. Big fat hardcover college-type books. Three of them. And a tiny paperback copy of *Winnie-the-Pooh*. She's got legs, too. Boy, does she have legs.

You'd think with all that's going on in my head about my damn father and what is going to happen to me and my mom I wouldn't be thinking about mating, but that's not how my brain works.

"This seat isn't taken, right?" I ask after I am already comfortably seated.

She says nothing.

A little while later I say, "Where you headed? I'm going to Baltimore."

Totally ignores me.

Newark, Philadelphia, Wilmington pass by, each with a lame attempt by yours truly at conversation.

She has mostly been looking out the window the entire trip. The few times she does look at me, I quickly turn away. I tell myself the next time she looks at me I won't do that. But I can't help it. I'm a goddamn idiot.

Finally, when she pulls back her hair the way pretty girls often do, I can see that she's been listening to her iPod all his time. She's got earphones in those perfect ears, hiding behind her shampoo-commercial flowing long blond hair.

It occurs to me I could say anything I want to her right now. Anything. So I do.

"I love you, strange, beautiful, unattainable woman. I must have you."

She just keeps looking out the window.

4

I wake up. My brain is all fuzzy. I have no idea where I am. When did I doze off? Did I miss my stop? Am I coming or am I going? Most important, where did Strange Beautiful Unattainable Woman go? Aha. We are pulling into Penn Station in Baltimore. Not to be confused with Penn Station in New York, where I started the trip. There are lots of people in the aisle waiting to bolt when the train doors open.

I don't see Strange Beautiful Unattainable Woman anywhere. She has taken all her books. So either she moved to some other car on the train or she is getting off in Baltimore. She could be up ahead in that long line of people waiting to exit.

I look down and at my feet lies her copy of *Winnie-the-Pooh*. She must have dropped it stepping over my dumb sleeping ass. I have to get it back to her.

I hope I wasn't snoring.

The train stops. The doors open. I rush out to the platform and spot her a ways ahead going up the stairs. I frantically follow.

An old lady built like a fire hydrant is keeping me from my destiny. She is walking very slowly and is incredibly hard to get around. When I go left, so does she. When I go right, so does she.

Damn. My dream woman is getting away.

Left with no other choice, I hip-check the old broad as we get to the stairs. I leap past her. I look back to make sure she isn't seriously hurt. Her glasses are askew. She flips me the bird.

When I get to the top of the stairs there are tons of people all over the station. Strange Beautiful Unattainable Woman is now the proverbial needle in the haystack.

Just when I think all hope is lost, way up ahead I catch a glimpse of her.

And miraculously, like when Charlton Heston parts the Red Sea in that Bible movie I was sat in front of every Easter, the crowd separates, leaving a clear path of open space between me and her. We actually make eye contact and I swear she smiles at me.

I start walking toward her, almost running, and when I get halfway there—*bam!*—this huge dude slams into me from out of nowhere. I fall directly on my ass.

The lady I hip-checked is passing by me at that very moment. She looks at me on the floor and cackles wildly. I don't appreciate it.

It's not until the guy who knocked me over offers his hand to help me up that I see it is my goddamn uncle Anthony.

"Ha!" he laughs. "I still got it!"

"Very funny, fat man!"

He gives me a big hug.

He sheds a tear.

Uncle Anthony wasn't at the funeral. He is/was Dad's older brother. They hadn't spoken in forever.

"Sorry about your pop," he says.

Pop? Who says "pop"?

I just kind of stand there. Over his shoulder, through the glass doors of the train station, I see Strange Beautiful Unattainable Woman has gotten into a taxi. The cab takes off. Now *I* want to cry.

Uncle Anthony wipes the tear from his cheek, points at the book in my hand, and says, "Interesting choice in reading material." Then he chuckles.

"It's not mine."

He chuckles some more.

"Where are your bags?" he asks.

"Shit, shit, shit!"

5

I'm sitting at the kitchen table in a Baltimore Orioles T-shirt that is about a billion times too big for me. It's Uncle Anthony's circa a thousand years ago. It stinks of whatever he does for a living. Something with gas or oil or air-conditioning. All I have to do is read the square truck in the driveway and I could give you a better idea, but who really cares?

He lives in a tiny row house. Baltimore all the way. It even has the Formstone on the outside, which is some kind of fake brick the locals put over real brick about a hundred and something years ago. Inside, the place is sparse and fairly neat and was probably last decorated in 1958.

"Am I supposed to go out like this?" I say from somewhere inside my supersized getup.

"Eat your eggs," says Uncle Anthony. "They're getting cold."

"They already are cold."

"Ungrateful dog."

"Cold, but delicious," I say.

My uncle smiles. I almost do.

"I'm off to work," he says.

"What am I gonna do all day around here for two weeks?"

Uncle Anthony walks over to his turn-of-the-century fridge. Under a magnet for Bobo's Hot Wings, he removes a piece of paper that at one time must have resided in a tiny spiral notebook. He walks back over to me and holds the note two inches from my face.

"I got it covered," he growls.

I grab the page out of his hand.

"See you at dinner. I'm bringing home a bucket of chicken," he tells me.

"I'm a vegetarian."

"I don't think they have vegetables at Colonel Sanders."

"Get me a tub of mashed potatoes."

"You kill me, kid."

"Don't tempt me."

"Read that list immediately," says Uncle Anthony. He knows me well enough to know that if I don't do something the moment I am asked, odds are it won't get done at all.

"I will."

He lets out a giant burp and leaves.

I go back to bed, immediately.

6

When I wake up I actually read the piece of paper
Uncle Anthony handed me a mere five hours ago.
Yeah, I slept quite a while.

Day One: Choose a mission.
Day Two: Find the best pizza joint in town.
Day Three: Clean out the garage.
Day Four: Muck the stalls at Riverbend Farm.
Day Five: Read a complete book under a tree.
Day Six: Go to a place of worship and pray.
Day Seven: Go on seven job interviews.

Day Eight: Spend the day thinking big thoughts. Write them down.
Day Nine: Eat a meal with a stranger.
Day Ten: Make me something.
Day Eleven: Recite a poem at Blake's Coffee Shop Midnight Poetry Reading.
Day Twelve: Complete your mission.

I'm not sure what to think about it. But it definitely makes me want to go back to bed.

So I do.

7

My dad is holding my Nintendo game console over his head at the top of the stairs.

"If you don't stop crying, I'm throwing this down to the bottom. One . . . Two . . ."

I start crying harder. He flings my best friend in the world to its certain death. I can't look. I close my eyes tight.

Bang, boom, crack, bam, boom.

The horror.

I wake up in a sweat. It was just a dream. But it really did happen. I was about seven and my dad was only a best-selling self-help-book author at the time. It was still years before he would become a daytime-TV-talk-show-host phenomenon.

I smell the deep-fried flesh of a bird murdered American-factory-style. That can only mean one thing: Uncle Anthony has arrived back home with food.

"So, Mr. Fathead, what did you do all day... sleep?"

"What if I did, Butterball?"

"I bet you didn't even read the list, did you, Stinky McStinky?"

"Really. Well, try this on for size: Strange Beautiful Unattainable Woman."

"If you just called me what I think you did—them is fighting words."

"I'm telling you what my mission will be: to find the strange, beautiful, unattainable woman I met on the train and return *Winnie-the-Pooh* to her."

"If that's what floats your boat, Bub."

"It floats it."

8

The day starts out with one bad thing after another:

1. I wake up grumpy and dead set against doing anything on my uncle's list that doesn't involve tracking down my dream woman.
2. I get into an argument with my uncle about his second task for me: to "find the best pizza joint in town."
3. He yells.
4. I yell.
5. We both yell simultaneously.

6. It gets so heated he throws an Eggo at me.
7. It is loaded with so much maple syrup that it sticks to my forehead for a good seven seconds.
8. I tell my uncle he can shove his silly list.
9. I leave in a huff.

9

I am running faster than I have ever run in my life. But the dogs are gaining on me just the same.

I have no idea where I am. But I'm not on the Upper West Side anymore, that is for damn sure.

The buildings are run-down. Many are boarded up. No one is around. Not a Starbucks in sight.

I'm pretty sure that at least three of the dogs are pit bulls.

The beasts are barking and growling and snarling, and as I look back they are less than fifty feet behind me.

I may have just pissed my pants.

What happened was that after I left Uncle Anthony's I got on the number 11 bus back to Penn Station with the copy of *Winnie-the-Pooh* and a plan to find my dream woman.

As soon as I sat down a dude one seat back asked me where I was going. I told him. The rest of the ride he kept yapping about how he knew me, that I was famous, that he saw me on TV. He stank of liquor. I ignored him until he yelled, "Get off here, kid! This is your stop! Get off here!"

I got off. Took a few wrong turns. Next thing I knew a huge canine with huge canines was chasing me. Then another dog joined in. Then another. Soon there were, like, half a dozen.

Which brings me to where I am now. Running my ass off.

The damn dogs are like twenty feet behind me. Their spittle is practically hitting the back of my All-Stars. These are not the proper shoes to be wearing if you are being hunted down by a pack of wild dogs, I'll tell you that. While you were reading that last sentence the dogs have closed in. They are ten feet behind me and gaining fast. I'm so out of shape. I've got nothing left. I'm huffing and puffing like a son of a gun.

Arruuugggghhhh.

I just got bit on the ass. Hopefully I sustained only wardrobe damage. I turn around. The mongrels back me against a wall.

I'm doomed.

A door opens to my right. A girl jumps out. Puts herself between them and me and yells as loud as a human can.

"Get the fuck out of here!"

The dogs look at her like she is out of her mind. They look at one another. Then at her. Then at one another. Then they flee.

"Motherfucking dogs—you okay?"

"How the hell did you do that?" I ask.

"Just gotta show them who's boss," she says with a strong Baltimore accent.

She is short, skinny, and has a round face that is pretty much filled up with two huge brown eyes, and short shiny black hair. Her mouth is tiny, but her lips are puffy. I'm guessing she's seventeen. She's beautiful in an angelic sort of way. I'm also sure she could take me in a fight.

"Well, thanks," I say. "You pretty much saved my life."

"Fucking eh, I did."

"Yep, fucking eh," I agree.

"Why are you wearing such a giant shirt?" she asks.

"To cover up where the dog bit me," I say.

I hold up my shirt to show her my butt.

"Nice," she says. "You better come in and let me take care of that."

"I think he just got my jeans. I'm fine."

"Sure you don't want me to make sure?"

"Well, um, well, I . . ."

She laughs, high and squeaky.

"I'm joking with you, dude."

I blush. I goddamn blush.

Made a fool of, I change the subject.

"Do you know where Penn Station is?"

"You're not from around here. I like that."

She grabs me by the collar, pulls me to her, and plants this amazing kiss on me. I feel it in every part of my body. Like the time I stuck a fork in a light socket. Knocked my socks off.

Wow.

She goes back in. Leaves me on the sidewalk in a daze.

Pops her head back out.

"Five blocks in the direction you came from and then right for three blocks."

"Huh?" I ask in a more moronic voice than I normally speak with.

"The way to Penn Station. Five blocks that way, then three to your right. You can't miss it."

I start heading off as she has ordered.

"You're not going back home from whence you came, are you?"

"Nope."

"Good, because we open at noon every damn day of the week. First slice is on me."

"Slice?" I say in my head.

I look up. There's a big sign. JOE AND TONY'S FAMOUS PIZZERIA.

Lordy.

I found the best pizza joint in Baltimore, after all. And it has nothing to do with the food.

10

"Did anyone come looking for a copy of *Winnie-the-Pooh?*" I ask.

"Winnie the who?" says the tall redheaded dude behind the window.

I'm at Penn Station. Talking to the guy who apparently is in charge of lost items. But I get the feeling this isn't a specialized position. What I know for certain is that this man is not taking his job seriously.

"Pooh," I say. "Winnie-the-Pooh."

"Did you just say poo? Poo? You just said poo!"

He gets all hysterical with laughter. Brilliant sense of humor, this guy has.

"C'mon, man, this is important."

"You sure you didn't leave it in the men's room? That's where most people leave their poo, you know."

He laughs even harder at that one. But once he sees the steam coming out of my ears, he abruptly stops.

"We don't have no *Winnie-the-Pooh* here. But you are the second one today who asked about it."

"Really? What did she look like?"

"Blond. Tall. And had a handlebar mustache..."

My face goes from anxious to confused to angry in a millisecond.

"Yep, she was a he."

"Damn."

"He was checking for his daughter. She came in from New York yesterday."

"Bingo. Did he leave a number where they could be reached?"

"No."

"Can I leave mine?"

"You could leave the book. That's the right thing to do. But I can tell there is love at stake here. And I firmly come down on the side of love. Hopefully he, or better yet she, checks back in with me."

"You are a good man, sir."

"You are not the first to say so."

11

I head out of Penn Station. Sitting on floor to the right of the exit doors is a homeless dude. I smelled him way before I saw him.

As I push the door open to get out of the place I turn my head in his direction.

He barks at me. Not a ferocious bark. A happy bark. Like a puppy dog.

I meow back and get the hell out of there.

12

"Pass the peas," I say.

"Wait, so you aren't going back to see the girl at the pizza joint?" asks Uncle Anthony.

"Nope."

"I don't get you, kid."

"It was perfect. I don't wanna mess that up."

"You are afraid of her, aren't you?"

"Little bit."

"HAAA!" laughs my uncle. He slams his fist on the table.

"But mostly I am in love with Strange Beautiful Unattainable Woman, anyway."

"Strange Beautiful Unattainable Woman Who You Will Never See Again, you mean. No girl like that, a college girl, is going to mess with some kid."

"I'm on her trail, dude. I left my number at the Lost and Found for her."

"Did you ask about your bag?"

"Shit, I forgot."

"You look ridiculous in my shirts and that one pair of jeans."

"I know. Plus, look at this."

I show my uncle the hole in my pants.

"Put that ass back on that chair, boy! I don't need to see that."

"I said, pass the peas."

"Only if you are cleaning the garage tomorrow."

"I am. I'm completing every mission on your silly list after all."

"Good boy, good boy. I only came up with it to keep you from being bored like the last time you stayed over."

"I was like eleven, man."

"You needed a list then and you need a list now."

"Well, today your list was magical, and I don't see how I can fight magic."

"Plus, what the hell else are you gonna do in this town?" says my uncle.

"That, too."

13

Uncle Anthony and I are watching TV in his dark, dank living room. We are watching some lame entertainment-magazine show. The square-jawed host says: "And next, a tribute to a great man. Someone the whole country loved, Dr. Frank Martin!"

They flash a picture of my dad on the screen. In the shot his arm is around me. It was taken a couple of years ago when he did a show about fathers and sons. The media have been using that photo in more than a few stories they have done on my dad's death. It makes him look like he was some kind of father of the year or something. Like we actually had a relationship. Makes my skin crawl. The camera pushes in tight on his smiling face.

"Ass!"

We say it simultaneously, Uncle Anthony and I.

We do have something in common, it turns out.

14

There is a little boy. He is crying. In pain. The kid is in his diapers. He might even be hurt. Almost everyone in the photograph is rushing toward the child. They look alarmed.

There is a man. Nicely dressed. Holding a drink. He is laughing. Talking to an older woman and her young, very pretty daughter. (The look in his eye tells you he has slept with one of them. Probably both.) They seem to be in their own bubble. Unaware of the crying boy, the others around them.

The boy is me. The man, my dad.

Perfect, right?

This is the image they should be blasting over the damn airwaves.

The photo was in a huge box I was stacking up in Uncle Anthony's garage. There were a few other photos of Mom and Dad and me in there. One of my mom, she must be my age in the picture, in a bathing suit, laughing with a skinny boy who looks like my dad a little, but I'm pretty sure is not. I take it.

Later, I ask Uncle Anthony if I can keep it.

He goes pale for a second, but then gives me a quick "Yep."

15

Horses are running everywhere. We are in the jeep chasing them through streets. Through other people's farms. Through hell and high water, really.

All I thought I was going to be doing all day was shoveling the shit, literally and otherwise.

Uncle Anthony made a big deal about how this would clear my head. He said he goes to the farm and mucks stalls when he is under stress. When he leaves, he says, he is a new man.

The ol' burly Riverbend Farm guy stops in the

middle of an open field, and he and I hop out and run toward some crazy-ass happy-to-be-free horses. Each of us has a bunch of halters in his hands and a determined look on his face. Frankly, I have no idea what I am doing. I'm using the monkey-see, monkey-do approach to horse handling.

Apparently, Uncle Anthony had to beg this dude to let me work at the farm for a day. The guy, his high school buddy, is very picky about what he calls "civilians" working at his place. They make him nervous. And the guy is due any day now for his fourth heart attack, Uncle Anthony warns, so I need to be on my best behavior.

The ol' guy is heaving and ho-ing along in front of me when out of nowhere he trips and falls. I hit the deck next to him.

"You didn't just have a heart attack, did you? Please don't do that!" I say, both of us still on the ground.

"What the hell were you thinking? Someone could get killed!"

"I wasn't thinking."

"Idiot!" he yells. "Who the hell leaves a damn gate open!"

I was in a complete funk, what can I say. I forgot to close a gate from which a large number of horses escaped. A gaggle of them, perhaps.

Kind of understandable from my point of view. I had just gotten a text from Strange Beautiful Unattainable Woman.

meet me @ penn 2morrow @ 1. dont 4get my book. :) thelma

Except for the disturbing combination of letters, numbers, and symbols, and the name Thelma, it was the greatest text I ever received.

A horse jumps over us. Pretty freaky. We get up and chase after it.

Once we get every one of them rounded up, they send me home. No one was hurt. Not a horse, not a human, not a car, nothing.

If I don't say anything to Uncle Anthony, they won't say anything to Uncle Anthony.

Plus, I am never to be allowed back on the farm again or ol' burly Riverbend Farm guy will personally take me apart limb by limb.

That's an easy deal for me to make.

16

10:00 a.m. I'm freakin' three hours early. A bit anxious, I'd say.

I got all dressed up. In other words, I'm wearing the same clothes I arrived at this fair city in. And they are washed. Duct-taped my jeans as well. I can't sew. Plus, Uncle Anthony didn't have needle and thread at his crib.

My assignment is to read a book under a tree. Well, there is a tree over there, and a bench, just feet from the side entrance to Penn Station, and I have her copy of *Winnie-the-Pooh* handy. It's as good a book as any.

I sit down and read.

The writing is actually pretty brilliant.

I'm enjoying this.

When I get to the end of the book I am very satisfied. Like a bear who has just finished the last pawful of honey from a healthy-size pot.

I smack my lips a few times and doze off for a few minutes.

17

It is Christmas morning. Mom and Dad are dressed as elves. They are standing in front of a perfectly decorated tree. Between them is a giant box with a big red bow.

They gesture for me to come to them. When I get there they point to the box.

I go to it and undo the bow. I flip off the lid and peer inside. A puppy. We all laugh.

My mom picks me up and puts me in the box with the dog.

I smile. The dog growls. Suddenly, his sweet face turns into my dad's face. He growls at me again.

This wakes me up. I hate the dreams I've been having lately.

I'm on the bench outside Penn Station. But now that fat homeless guy from the other day is sitting next to me. He growls. Then he starts barking. His stink is all over me. I run back into Penn Station.

My God. It is 1:27. Holy crap. All this stress is turning me into a sleepaholic.

I look around but Strange Beautiful Unattainable Woman is nowhere to be found. Maybe she's out there looking for me. I'll hold up *Winnie-the-Pooh* and jump around like a complete ass. That will make a great impression.

Goddamn it. The book! Where the hell is the book?

I run back outside to the bench. Homeless guy is on his back, sprawled all over it. You can barely even tell a bench is there at all.

I'm guessing the book is somewhere under him. A horrible thought.

I have another horrible thought. I have to reach under him and pull that book out. I have to, god-damn it.

He is damp. And greasy. I am going to need a shower or two after this. Three showers. And one of those hose-downs they give you after you come in contact with radioactive materials.

I'm reaching under him and I can't seem to locate the book.

He yawns loudly, and stretches and arches his back for a second. I reach a little farther in and I'm pretty sure my fingertips touch *Winnie-the-Pooh*.

I

almost

have

it.

Homeless dude slams his back down on my arm. He sneezes. A wet one. I nearly vomit.

The book has scooted farther away. Worse than that, I can't get my limb out from under this dude.

Shit, he smells awful.

I turn around to see if anyone can help me out of this predicament. Through the glass door I see

Strange Beautiful Unattainable Woman inside Penn.

She is walking away from me. She stops. Checks her watch. Looks surprised, like she just remembered she was late for another appointment, and runs out of view.

My heart sinks. I can only guess she is headed to the door on the opposite side of the station.

I squirm and shove and push and wiggle.

"Sir! Could you . . ."

I put my feet up against the edge of the bench, butt in the air, and push off as hard as I possibly can. I fly backward on my ass and do two complete tuck-and-rolls before I come to a stop, without the damn book.

I leap to my feet and head back inside the train station.

I run to the middle of the place and spin around like a top, trying to spot her.

Penn is pretty empty now. It must be ugly hour because it is like *Dawn of the Dead* in here.

My pocket buzzes. I pull out my phone. A text.

where were u? i waited a half hour. had 2 go.
i have something 4 u 2 make u :)

I sit down. Not knowing if I'm happy or sad. But certain that I want something from her that will make me :).

I can only hope we are thinking of the same thing.

18

I go back out to the bench. The homeless guy is gone. The book is too.

My phone buzzes again. Another text. It must be her!

Herc, call me! Love, Mom

Not what I was hoping for.

The phone buzzes once more. Now this has to be her.

*c u after work 2morrow. dinner@ 7. u name
the place. bring pooh.*

That's her all right.

Bring *Pooh*, my ass. Gotta find that bear and
bum.

19

"You seriously spent the day looking for a homeless man?"

"Yes, Uncle Fat Ass, that is what I did."

"You've really hit rock bottom, boy. You went from searching for the most beautiful girl in the world to not finding someone most people would avoid at all costs."

"Well, he has the book, dumbass."

"Temper, temper."

"I had a rough day. That crazy dude disappeared and he took my girl's book with him!"

"Hee-hee. Your girl. Good one."

"He's basically the size of a planet. How can a major planet just go *poof!* I should have been able to locate him by his stench alone!"

"So he is about the same size as a planet? And he smells like Uranus?"

"You're so funny."

"Well, I know that you are the brilliant one and I am the dumbass, but why didn't you just buy the same book at the bookstore and give that to her?"

My brain nearly explodes right there on the spot.

"I never thought I'd say this, but I love you, Uncle Anthony."

"You are really going soft, Herc. It is sad to witness."

"Don't look."

"I won't," he says.

20

I'm about to finish my third appetizer.

"Are you sure your guest is coming, sir?" the waiter asks me.

I'm sure I look miserable. That's about the only thing I'm sure of.

I don't really say yes or no. Luckily, the waiter feels sorry for me and nods his head politely, then quickly heads back to wherever it is waiters go when they aren't attending to their tables.

Is this some kind of punishment for me not meeting her at Penn Station? I must look ridiculous to everyone else in the place. Me in my jeans and an oversize Winston cigarette shirt that they must have awarded Uncle Anthony because he smoked the most cartons in the Mid-Atlantic region for three years in a row or something. Everyone else in their yuppie polo shirts and khakis and Laura Ashley sundresses. Where the hell are my clothes anyway?

Oh my God. There they are. My clothes. Well, my favorite shirt, anyway. At the front of the restaurant.

Waving to me.

Coming toward me.

It kisses me on the cheek.

Sits down across from me.

It looks damn good.

"I see your guest has made it," says the waiter, who must have come over while I was fixated on the amazing entrance of Strange Beautiful Unattainable Woman.

sigh

21

"How did you know it was me?" I ask, since I don't think we ever actually made eye contact on the train.

"How did I know?" she says.

"So you did notice me on the train? I thought you were in your own little iPod world. But you did notice me."

"I did."

"And you thought I was cute?"

"Ha." She laughs. Then she winks.

That's not terrible, I think.

"Like my shirt?" she asks.

"Yeah, I do."

"I picked it up when some loser stood me up at Penn Station. The guy at the station wasn't going to give it to me at first but he said he would make an exception because he could see love was involved. I told him I just wanted some leverage to get my book back."

She slams my bag in my lap. I put it under my seat.

"Speaking of your book, here you go," I say.

I hand it to her.

She tosses it into her purse.

"Dinner is on me!" she blurts out.

"No, it is on me," I say.

"On me. I want to thank you."

"No, on me."

"Is that because you are the man and I am the little lady? How 1950s of you!"

"I just want to pay is all."

"Well, whoever pays, the other one orders the food. The power must be shared."

"Hmmm," I muse.

"It is only fair."

"Fine," I say. "I'll pay, you order."

Bad idea.

She orders.

Not a single animal is left off her killing spree. She orders chicken and beef and pig and lamb. The beef is raw.

I just grin. Like the ass I am.

I swear I hear the pork chop squeal as she bites into it.

The chicken wings try to run off her plate, but she stabs them with her fork right before they make it to freedom.

Whenever she daintily dabs her mouth with her napkin, I imagine she is wiping away blood.

The lamb kebabs just look into my eyes and whimper, knowing their fate is sealed.

And she does it all in slow motion. Her every carnivorous move is pure poetry.

For my part, I dig right in. I clear my plate with gusto. As if to say, I'm a goddamn man, Thelma. An animal such as yourself, but more so. Hear me roar, Thelma. Hear me roar.

Frankly, I think I may have actually roared out loud at one point. But I can't be sure. Because the visuals in my head were so vibrant. So fantastic. I know we spoke, and smiled at each other, and even laughed at times, I just don't remember what we were saying. Even as it was happening.

We were connecting. I know that.

22

After dinner she takes me to her favorite place in the world.

Riverbend Farm.

She takes riding lessons there.

It is night, probably close to eleven, and no one is around. We are in the main barn.

"I love animals, especially horses," she says.

I think back to dinner. The thought amuses me. I think about saying "Because they are so tasty?" but I decide against it.

"I love to come here at night, just me and the horses. It is so spiritual, you know?"

"I do," I say. But of course, I don't.

"My God, it is magnificent." She takes a deep breath and her eyes wander around the joint. "It is so fitting that horses live in a building that feels so much like a church, don't you think?"

This barn is a stellar piece of architecture, I must admit. With its high ceiling and tall windows and woodwork, it is churchlike.

She grabs my hand and takes me over to the hugest horse in the place.

"This is Canosa," she says. "He is the high priest."

"He looks really old. Really old."

"He is wise. I confess all my sins to him. And he absolves me."

I think about Thelma's sins.

Then I lean in for a kiss. She leans in too.

Before our lips meet, I get a flashback of Uncle Anthony saying, "No girl like that, a college girl, is going to mess with some kid."

For a fraction of a fraction of a second I question Thelma's motives.

But then our lips lock and I know this is right.

23

Quick prayer: **Thank you, Lord.** Thank you. Amen.

This the part of the movie where they cut away to a waterfall or something.

We are rounding second base. Going for third. The coach in my head is giving me the stop sign, but I may just run through it.

You shouldn't be here.

Plus I have no idea what I am doing. I'm awkward and uncoordinated and unsure of every move I am making.

It feels like it is going well, though. But I thought the same thing about my end-of-the-year oral report on World War II, and I flunked that pretty badly. So be on your way. Nothing to see here. Scat.

24

I wake up in a pile of straw. Thelma is wrapped around me. It is the next morning. Early. Very early.

I don't want to ever leave this place. But on the other hand, if I get seen at Riverbend Farm, my ass is grass. And I hear vehicles driving up outside.

I try to wake Thelma up. No dice.

I pick her up and I carry her to the barn door. When I open it I come face-to-face with ol' burly round Riverbend Farm guy.

I am so dead.

He looks pretty shocked to see me. He grabs me by the front of my hair and tugs. Then he pinches my left cheek and twists it a bit.

"Way to go, kid. You done good."

He gives me the thumbs-up and a devilish grin. He gives Thelma, still out like a light, an utterly filthy look. Then he giggles like a schoolgirl and walks off. Men like when men score. It is one of the rare times we actually pull for one another. But in this case it is creepy as shit.

I take Thelma's keys, start up her car, and get us the hell out of there.

It is nice to be behind the wheel, instead of on a bus or in the back seat of a cab for once. But while I drive off into the morning my eyes are barely on the road ahead of me.

Thelma is the most beautiful girl on the planet.

25

My uncle is standing in front of me and full-out blubbering, sniffling, spitting, nose-running, red-faced, hysterical bawling his eyes out. It is funny and tragic all at once. It's also kind of scary because I have no idea where it is coming from.

When I got to Uncle Anthony's house I was certain he would (A) have already left for work and (B) have figured there was no need to bother his hard-sleeping nephew, who was apparently out like a light behind the closed door of his bedroom.

Neither was true.

When I arrived, his square work truck was in the driveway. This puzzled me but not enough to keep me from putting my key in the door, opening it up, and letting myself in. Next thing I knew I was face-to-face with the guy. And he was already in the sorry state I described a few sentences ago.

"Why, why, why, why, why, why!" was the beginning of his long diatribe. Only every fifth phrase or so was audible. Some of the phrases I did pick up were "I worry," "your mother," "doing my best." And it all ended with "I'm going through a lot here, man!"

Really? He is going through a lot? News to me. And what about all I'm going through?

I explain that it was fine. That I was with Strange Beautiful Unattainable Woman and her family. (Those horses are her family, right?) That we talked all night and fell asleep and her family was fine with it all.

Still teary-eyed, but much more under control, my uncle makes me promise to finish my tasks. He says that they will keep me out of trouble. And swears it will all make sense in the end.

Which is crazy, because I had begun to wonder

why I was doing them at all. I had only a few minutes ago, on the way home, told myself that I was done with the silly game, especially since I had found my unattainable woman and become one with her.

I just look at him, stunned by the whole scene.

"Please, just do this for me."

"I will," I say.

Then he asks me if I have completed all the tasks so far, including yesterday's task of going to a place of worship and praying.

I tell him that I have.

Because I have.

26

I've probably only been asleep five minutes or so when I suddenly spring out of bed.

Shit, I have no idea where I left my bag! Did I leave it at the restaurant? The farm? Probably the restaurant. I am certainly not going back to the farm!

It only takes a second for the irrational panic to subside. My mind quickly turns to the thought of a giant bowl of guacamole. Seconds later I am sleeping like a baby.

27

Job interview day. I decide to have fun with it.

I go into the Starbucks and ask for an application.

On the line where they ask for my name I write, "Juan Valdez."

On the line where they ask what compensation I want I write, "Only the finest hand-picked Colombian coffee beans."

"So, Juan, why do you want to work at Starbucks?" asks the dude interviewing me. He is tall and white all over. Translucent skin. He has a huge super-blond Afro. I have no idea how old he is but he looks like he could be my age.

"The girls," I say.

He just looks at me with his mouth open.

"The chicks, man," I say. "All the hot chicks ordering all the frou-frou soy sugar-free frappawhatevers."

I see a light go off in his head.

"Dude, dude, dude, that is exactly why I work here!"

"Dude!" I say, and I give him a little slug on the arm.

"Dude!" he says, giving me one back.

I lean in and whisper, "Dude," pointing my head in the direction of a girl who has just walked in.

He turns around, checks her out, and smiles.

He turns back to me, wiggling his barely noticeable eyebrows up and down, Groucho Marx style.

"Duuuuuuuuuuuuude," he chuckles.

I get the job.

28

I go into the McDonald's and ask for an application.

On the line where they ask for my name I write, "Phil O. Phisch."

In the section where they ask what position you are looking for I check the box for cook, but under it in all caps I write: "I WANT THE CLOWN'S JOB!"

"You can't have the clown's job," says the red-headed lady interviewing me. She is fifty-ish, I'm guessing. Tiny pug nose. Buckteeth. All of that going against her and she still winds up being strangely attractive.

"Can't you see I want his job?" she adds, flicking her bright frizzy locks.

"What about the Hamburglar? Is that position filled yet?"

"Yes, strangely enough it is filled by the Hamburglar himself."

"Hmmmmm. I thought he might have been serving time in the state pen by now."

"What about assistant manager?" she asks me.

"Seriously? Based on that application?"

"Look, kid, you are smart and funny." Then she jokes that I am also tall enough to reach the napkins on the top shelf of the storage closet.

I don't know what to say. I just sit there like a dummy in my triple-XL Natty Boh T-shirt.

She asks me if I can start tomorrow.

No can do.

29

I go into a **Super Tan** and ask for an application.

On the line where they ask for my name I write, "Mel Anoma."

In the section where they ask you to write down your hobbies I write, "Baking."

"So, like, Mel, like, we really, like, don't have any openings and all, but, like, even if we, like, did, we only hire hot girls mostly, and well, like, you are not a hot girl and stuff, so, like, you might just want to, like, not bother with Super Tan and all," is what

I expect the blond babe interviewing me to say. But she is not what I assumed.

She is actually a brainiac with perfect diction.

She is tall and busty, with her long hair pulled back in a ponytail. She is wearing a shirt that shows off her very tight tummy. Naturally, she is tan. Well, probably unnaturally tan. But the point is she is a life-size bronzed Barbie doll.

A very smart life-size bronzed Barbie doll. I learn of her superior intellect when, as a way to make the interview more conversational, I ask about the philosophy book on her desk. She jumps right in, excited that I am interested, and starts talking way over my head. Occasionally when she mentions a philosopher or a theory or whatever, I pretend to know what she is talking about. It only takes a few additional words for her to realize I am a fraud. But she humors me. Eventually all I can do is laugh and smile and gaze into her eyes.

I am the dumb blond in this scenario.

She really seems to like talking to me, though. The interview lasts a solid hour.

She shakes my hand and says, "I will be in touch."

When I look back in the picture window after leaving, I see her pick up the application and read it for the first time. She laughs.

Five minutes later she calls and offers me the job.

30

I go on three more interviews.

They all go really well. I am apparently very charismatic. This is something I did not know about myself. Maybe it is because I feel no pressure to please, since there is nothing on the line. I do not want the jobs and will probably never see these folks again. It is liberating as shit, actually.

I have called Thelma between each and every interview and she has not picked up. I call again. Still no answer.

Frankly, I am surprised she hasn't called me.

I demand my phone to ring. I stare it down.

To my surprise, it rings. I have won the battle of wills.

But not so fast. The call is not from Thelma. It is my mom.

I do not pick up. That would be admitting defeat.

Instead, I stare the dastardly device down harder.

After about nine minutes of nothing happening, we both agree to call it a draw.

31

I walk into Jerry's Taxi Service and ask for an application.

"We don't take applications," says the very old dude behind the counter.

I do a quick twirl and head in the reverse direction toward the door.

"Where the hell you going?" yells the old man as my hand touches the doorknob.

I keep my body where it is but turn my head in his direction.

"You said you don't have any openings, man."

"What I said was we don't take applifuckingcations, but we always have openings."

"I see, so what is the procedure, then?"

"You get your ass over here and I ask you Jerry's Taxi's three questions."

I walk over.

"Shoot."

"Question number one: Best all-time shortstop?"

The place is covered in Orioles memorabilia.

"Cal Ripken," I say.

"Question number two: Greatest film director?"

"John Waters," I say, sticking with the Baltimore theme.

"Question number three: A. Crabs, B. Duckpin bowling, C. Screen painting, D. Formstone, or E. None of the above."

I have no idea where he is going with this one but I blurt out, "Letter B!" not even remembering what answer that corresponds with.

Long silence.

"How'd I do?" I ask.

"Belanger, Levinson, and All of the above. You got every fucking one wrong."

"All of the above wasn't even an option," I yell as I head toward the door.

"Sometimes your only option when driving a cab is something you didn't think was an option at all."

"That is the most ridiculous test I have ever taken."

"Well, it got you hired, boy!"

"C'mon, old dude," I say. "Really?"

"Come back and meet the gang."

The gang?

32

There are beers, a couple of cabbies who have just finished their shift, and three tough-looking women in full Roller Derby gear.

What started as the elderly guy introducing me to my fellow cabbies has turned into a decent party, and I am at the center of it all.

We are in the back room of Jerry's Taxi Service. I am having the time of my life until one of the girls whispers into my ear:

"Sid almost didn't hire you, but then he recognized you from the TV."

I can barely believe what I just heard.

I don't even say it out loud. I just look her in the face and mouth, "What?"

"Sid ain't never had a celebrity work here," she says.

I can't totally explain it, but I go ballistic. I jump out of my chair and let out a very high-pitched yell. I throw my beer can across the room. I jump up and down in place, waving my arms like a maniac. They all just stare at me until one of my hands accidentally slaps one of the girls on the back of the head. She jumps me. Next thing I know I am rolling around the place with three Roller Derby gals.

They mop the floor with me.

I twist my ankle pretty badly in the brawl.

I will probably have a black eye.

I am fired.

33

When I limp in at dinnertime Uncle Anthony doesn't even make eye contact with me. He is still too embarrassed to talk about his blubbering. I am too embarrassed to talk about my ass getting whupped.

In Man World, it is proper to wait a day or two to face each other after such incidents. And the incidents are never to be brought up in conversation. Never.

I put a frozen bean burrito in the microwave and

grab a bottle of water out of the fridge. When the timer goes off I get my Mexican treat and smother it with hot sauce. I take it straight to my bedroom.

I practically swallow it whole.

After a few minutes I try to think whether it tasted good or not.

It doesn't matter. I am too tired to care.

I sleep like a baby.

34

It is a beautiful morning. Well, it is actually a tad after noon. And yeah, my eye is puffy and my ankle is black-and-blue, but I seem to have woken up on the right side of the bed.

I sit on a park bench and write down big thoughts:

Things would be better if pigs ruled the world.

Baseball games are too long. Outlawing spitting and scratching one's crotch would cut off a few minutes from each game.

War is bad, peace is good.

*If humans are more evolved than chimps,
how come chimps are the ones that have feet
that work as well as hands?*

*On second thought, things would be better if
dolphins ruled the world.*

Then I start making predictions:

*Life will be discovered in another universe in
my lifetime.*

I will wind up marrying Thelma.

We will live in a brick ranch-style home.

*I will build Thelma a fountain on our fifth
anniversary. The fountain will be surrounded
by a small pond filled with goldfish. It will
not be as cheesy as you are thinking.*

We will have twelve kids. Enough to field

*two teams and a bench player for a game of
full-court basketball.*

*I will give my wife and children my undi-
vided attention.*

I will not be a dick.

35

Tht wz nt my book!!!!!!!!!!!!!!!!!!!!! Thelm

That is the text on my phone from Thelma.

Why would someone who has such an aversion to using unnecessary (actually necessary) letters deploy so many exclamation points?

She must be pissed.

36

"Of course she is mad at you. The book you gave her was an impostor, trash for brains," says Uncle Anthony.

"It was your idea, Bozo."

"That's Mr. Bozo to you. And it was just a suggestion."

"I'm getting her that book back if it's the last thing I do."

Uncle Anthony goes to the freezer. He takes out a steak, puts it on the table, and then slides it across to me the way a bartender slides a beer to a patron.

"I know you're a vegetarian but you may wanna put that on your shiner for a bit."

37

"Woof, woof," I say.

"Woof, woof?" answers the freckle-faced man behind the information counter at Penn Station.

"Yes, he woofs a lot and he is huge and smelly and he is here all the time."

"Oh yeah, Barky, love Barky. Nice, nice guy."

He checks his watch.

"Well, it's noon, so he is probably at the St. John's Homeless Shelter. They serve lunch."

"Address?"

"Just one block north on Charles."

I'm already out the door.

As I head down the street to retrieve my book I sing a happy tune that has been stuck in my head since I read *Pooh*:

"Cottleston, Cottleston, Cottleston Pie,
A fly can't bird, but a bird can fly.
Ask me a riddle and I reply
'Cottleston, Cottleston, Cottleston Pie.'"

38

There is a very, very long line going into the shelter. I run past it to the door. A huge dude stops me.

"Sir, you have to wait in line just like everyone else," says he.

"Oh, I'm not homeless," I say.

I look at myself through his eyes. I'm a skinny guy with an oversize Bertha's Mussels T-shirt, ripped jeans, a black eye, and a limp. If this was Halloween and there was a contest, first prize would go to James "Hercules" Martino for his realistic portrayal of one of the city's homeless folk.

"I'll just go to the back of the line," I say politely.

When I arrive there I start to get kind of anxious. I am a tad out of my element here. These are not my usual peeps.

I mutter my happy tune while I wait. Not only does this ease my mind but it helps me feel more like one of the guys.

39

"You are not going to say that! You are not going to say that!"

"Oh, I'm saying it, Bruce," I say. "And I will say it again, Julie Newmar is the best goddamn Catwoman of all time."

I am sitting at a table with a group of homeless guys. The conversation started when I got on the back of the line. They were discussing who the best James Bond was. Then who the best Batman was. Before I knew it we were debating the best Charlie's Angel to be stuck on a desert island with and someone was handing me a tray with a nice lunch on it. Since we sat down the conversation had changed to who was the best Catwoman.

Bruce is leading the Halle Berry camp. Willie and his boys are 100 percent behind Michelle Pfeiffer. I stand alone with Julie Newmar. She was the Catwoman in the old *Batman* TV show from the sixties or whenever. My dad loved it and bought the whole series on DVD. We would watch it together, over and over again.

Wow.

This is the first good memory of my dad I have had since he went kaput.

Right when the discussion starts getting quite heated, a booming voice comes from the back of the shelter.

"You're all wrong! It is Eartha Kitt!"

We turn around and it's Barky.

Barky comes over to our table. Plops his tray of food down. Pulls up a chair. He has on a big ol' army coat, and much to my delight, peeking out of the top pocket is Thelma's *Winnie-the-Pooh*.

We all chatter for a good hour and a half. Not once do I wonder how these guys wound up here.

No one talks about the war, or drugs, or beatings from the father who ruined their lives. I just have a really good time with a bunch of guys I had never met before.

I walk out of the place with Barky.

"I think you have my book," I say.

"No, I do not," says Barky.

"I can see it, man."

"No, you can't."

"Dude, it is right there, sticking out of your top pocket."

"This my book, kid."

"No, no."

"Yes, yes."

"No."

Instead of continuing on like this, I negotiate a price of forty bucks for it. Hey, Barky is a hard bargainer. But the important thing is I have the book.

I text Thelma immediately.

I stare at my phone.

Two minutes have gone by and she has not responded.

Now three.

Now four.

This goes on for three hundred and sixty more minutes.

Then this text:

Meet me in front of our restaurant at nine. Wear your Winston cigarette shirt. Your friend, Thelma

40

The first thing I do when I get to "our restaurant" is to see if they have my bag of clothes. They do not.

I go back outside. Wait for about fifteen minutes. Thelma is going to be very late, based on what I know of her. I may as well go in and get us a table. Maybe get an appetizer or two.

I tell the guy valet parking cars that if he sees a blonde with legs that don't quit waiting out here, to tell her Hercules is inside waiting for her.

"Hercules!" yells the valet guy. "Who is the girl—Cleopatra?"

Man, people do not know their Greek myths.

41

I'm about to finish my third appetizer.

"Are you sure your guest is coming, sir?" asks the same waiter we had last time in exactly the same way. I don't think he remembers me.

A few seconds later this girl is running at full speed straight toward my table. She sits down in my booth. She is freckled and dorky. But I can see how she could blossom into a supermodel if everything went just right.

"So you are Hercules," she says.

"Did something happen to Thelma?"

"Can I have one of those french fries?"

I push the plate toward her.

"Is Thelma okay?"

"She said you were cute. You're cute. What happened to your eye?"

I get angry. Or scared. I bang on the table.

"Is

Thelma

okay?"

Before she says anything it flashes before my eyes:

Thelma chasing a puppy across the street with a bus about to crush her.

Thelma's shoe getting stuck on a railroad track with a locomotive fast approaching. She is frantically attempting to unfasten its strap.

Thelma leans on the balcony of a forty-story hotel and it gives way. She is falling helplessly, at amazing speeds, to the ground.

"She is okay," interrupts the girl.

"What is going on here?" I ask.

"Listen, Thelma will probably kill me, but I'm going to be straight with you."

"Do that. Be straight with me."

"Okay, I'll come right out with it."

Long pause.

"C'mon, come right out with it," I prod.

"Thelma is a serial celebrity sleeper."

"She's a what?"

"A serial celebrity sleeper."

"A what?"

"She does it with famous people. She figures if she gets a decent amount of them she can write a blog about it and maybe get on a reality show at some point. She's only just started. She slept with a Justin Timberlake impersonator and you so far."

"Really, a Justin Timberlake impersonator?"

"Yeah, he was the first, even before she had the idea, and then she saw you on the train after seeing you on TV the day before, and the whole plan came to her in a flash. So she wrote her number in her book and left it on your lap and then you called her and then you did it and now you are here with me."

"She wrote her number in *Winnie-the-Pooh*?"

"Anyway, I was supposed to tell you that she was in a terrible accident and died or was in a coma or whatever. But we didn't really work out the details, and you turned all white and shit. Excuse my language."

She looks at her watch.

"Oh, I really have to go. Sorry about all this."

She gets up. Kisses me on the cheek. "Your father was a gift to the world. Thelma, especially, was a huge fan."

She leaves and it flashes before my eyes:

That bus smashes into Thelma.

The locomotive blows right over her.

Thelma plummets to the ground. Then *SPLAT.* Flat as a pancake.

42

That night I have a lot of dreams. But I can only remember two when I wake up.

The first dream is about that jar of pickles.

No one can open it. The grown-ups pass it around the table. Each one tries to open it. Each one fails. My dad goes next. He tries with all his might. His face goes red. But he cannot open the jar of pickles. He passes the jar to me. I must be about six years old. I grab it and twist as hard as I can. And it opens.

"Hercules!" my dad yells. "You did it!"

It is a dream of a story people have been telling me all my life. The story of how I got my name.

I have only a faint memory of the actual event. But I remember the cheers after my feat of strength. The pats on the back. The hugs. And then came the voice of my dad announcing, "I must have loosened it for the kid!"

From that point on he never let me feel good about any success I ever had. He was relentless. He was a fucking god and I was shit. After my twelfth birthday he just plain ignored me. Which, in a way, was worse.

I used to sit and cry in my room and wonder what the hell I did to make him hate me so damn much. When I was younger I was sure it was because I opened the pickle jar when he could not. If only I didn't show him up, then he would have loved me.

Shit.

Anyway.

In my second dream I am building the fountain that I had planned for Thelma. But I am building it for Cleopatra.

43

"A fountain with a pond?" asks the woman at Home Depot.

"Yes, one I can make in one day."

She sells me a kit. Looks simple enough.

Eight hours later I am totally frustrated with the project. The instructions are impossible.

All I have done is dug a very deep hole in my uncle's backyard. But someone is going to get a damn fountain. Anyone. And if it isn't Thelma or Cleopatra it may as well be my uncle.

So I'm in this hole and suddenly it starts raining.

Pouring. I try to get out as fast as I can and my legs go out from under me. I land flat on my back. I am in a hole in the ground. And I just lie there like a man in a grave.

For a moment I imagine I am my father. Just for a moment.

He would have killed in those job interviews, too, I think. That was him in me.

Lying there, for the first time I feel the loss. He was an ass, and I wasn't perfect, but if we had more time maybe we could have made things right.

I just lie there for twenty minutes.

The rain stops.

The sun comes out.

I go inside and make my uncle a cake.

It is not a fountain. But it will be delicious.

44

I sleep until about two in the afternoon, when my ringing cell phone wakes me up.

It is just my mom.

I hit MUTE, get out of bed, and get a drink of water.

I take a piss.

I go back to bed.

And don't wake up until the next day.

45

My vagina is killing me
My vagina aches
My vagina is asking me questions
And my breasts have no answers
But my buttocks tells no lies
Thank you, thank you very much.

That's the end of the twenty-seventh poem I have heard at Blake's Coffee Shop Midnight Poetry Reading. They all have been pretty much like this. Some were about death, and others seemed to be about death. That last one was the only one about talking vaginas. And death.

Mine is going to be a huge hit.

I head up to the stage.

"Hello, my name is Hercules Martino and I'd like to read a poem.

"Cottleston, Cottleston, Cottleston Pie,
A fly can't bird, but a bird can fly.
Ask me a riddle and I reply
'Cottleston, Cottleston, Cottleston Pie.'

"Cottleston, Cottleston, Cottleston Pie,
A fish can't whistle and neither can I.
Ask me a riddle and I reply
'Cottleston, Cottleston, Cottleston Pie.'

"Cottleston, Cottleston, Cottleston Pie,
Why does a chicken, I don't know why.
Ask me a riddle and I reply
'Cottleston, Cottleston, Cottleston Pie.'

"That's it. That's all I got."

My poem is met with a smattering of confused applause. Losers.

I head back to my seat.

Just when it looks like the night is over, a dark figure approaches from the very back of the place. Holy crap! It is Uncle Anthony. His hand is shaking as he takes a weathered piece of paper out of his top pocket. He begins reading. Slowly. Staring directly into my eyes.

"I still love her.
He took her from me.
When I was just a boy.
My own brother.
I never recovered.
I still love her.

"I still love her.
He took her from me.
Now you are a grown boy.
My nephew, my friend.
I need you to know.
I have always loved her.

"I still love her.
Your mother.

I did not know how to tell you.
In the language we have cultivated.
But I would burst if I did not say.
So I gave you twelve labors.
With the hope they would bring you here.
And so they have.

"I still love her.
He took her from me.
And now he from her.
But I have no move to make.
No grand gesture to take.
Except to say.
I have always loved her.

"I have only loved her."

Uncle Anthony puts his head down. Slowly exits stage left.

The crowd gives him a standing ovation.

Eventually, I do likewise. Crawling under my chair and curling up in the fetal position would have called too much attention to myself.

46

Over breakfast Uncle Anthony produces two tickets to the Orioles game for that afternoon.

We talk baseball the rest of the day.

We never mention my mother, or the poem, or anything.

We are men, after all.

47

"Take it easy, Ass-for-Brains," says my uncle.

"So long, ya jerk. I'll miss you."

The cabbie behind us starts honking his horn. I get out, walk up to the entrance of Penn Station, and turn around expecting to see the back of my uncle's truck making the turn onto Charles Street. But he hasn't moved an inch.

He waves.

The cabbie lays on his horn hard and long.

I wave.

My uncle heads out. I head in.

I check the big board and see that my train doesn't leave for forty-eight minutes.

I look around for Barky. No sign of him.

I'm starving. But Penn Station food isn't the best. Then I remember the best pizza place in Baltimore. I also remember the angel with the mouth of a truck driver.

I take off for Joe and Tony's Famous Pizzeria.

I make a few wrong turns, but I just keep running, hoping the next turn will make things right. Baltimore looks beautiful. The place has really grown on me. If it were raining this could be the last scene in a Hollywood romance.

I see the pizza joint up ahead.

I burst through the door of Joe and Tony's, and she is cleaning off a table.

I rush to her and plant one on her lips.

She slaps me.

Then she winks and giggles.

Her back is to a guy who must be a football lineman when he isn't making pizzas. He leaps over the counter.

"I will fucking kill you!"

I run out of the place.

Right behind me is the Incredible Hulk. I actually think he has gotten bigger and turned green since I last peeked back to get a look.

Behind him is the pizza girl, yelling, "No, Nino, no!"

The blood filling Nino's head with rage has apparently impaired his ability to hear.

"Run, out-of-towner, run!" yells the pizza girl.

Believe me, I am running as fast as I can.

I take this guy all over Baltimore. It is a complete tour. Shit, I am so lost. And tired. And the guy is right on my heels.

I make a right turn and suddenly Penn Station is directly in front of me.

As I make it inside I hear them announcing last call for the 96 Regional to New York.

This monster is right behind me as I head down the stairs.

Pizza Girl is bringing up the rear.

I get on the train. Damn. I did it. I haven't been torn limb from limb.

But this freaking moose just hops on the train, too.

He starts chasing me through the cars.

He gets a hold of my incredibly large T-shirt. The shirt rips and I burst out of the train and back onto the platform.

The train doors close.

Hulk is going to New York. He sticks his face against a window and makes angry gestures at me.

I wave good-bye to him.

Pizza Girl runs to my side, takes my hand, and waves good-bye to him as well.

48

Lily, that's the pizza girl's name, and I sit and talk while I wait for the next train.

That was her cousin chasing me. He is very protective. And has serious anger issues.

No kidding.

She says she has never just kissed a boy out of the blue until me. That she does believe in love at first sight. That she will come to New York to visit.

None of it may be true.

But I believe it.

49

I am on the train back to New York.

I take a window seat.

I stare out at the broken-down buildings and empty streets.

A stray kitten appears on a rooftop. I strain my neck to keep it in my sight for as long as I possibly can.

After a bit I start to doze off, scenes from the last two weeks overlapping in my brain.

I lean my seat back as far as it will go.

For a moment I feel myself in that hole in the ground again, the rain pouring down on me, in Uncle Anthony's backyard.

I'm slipping into sleep.

But before I'm totally out, my phone rings.

It is my mom.

I pick up.